W9-AQN-627

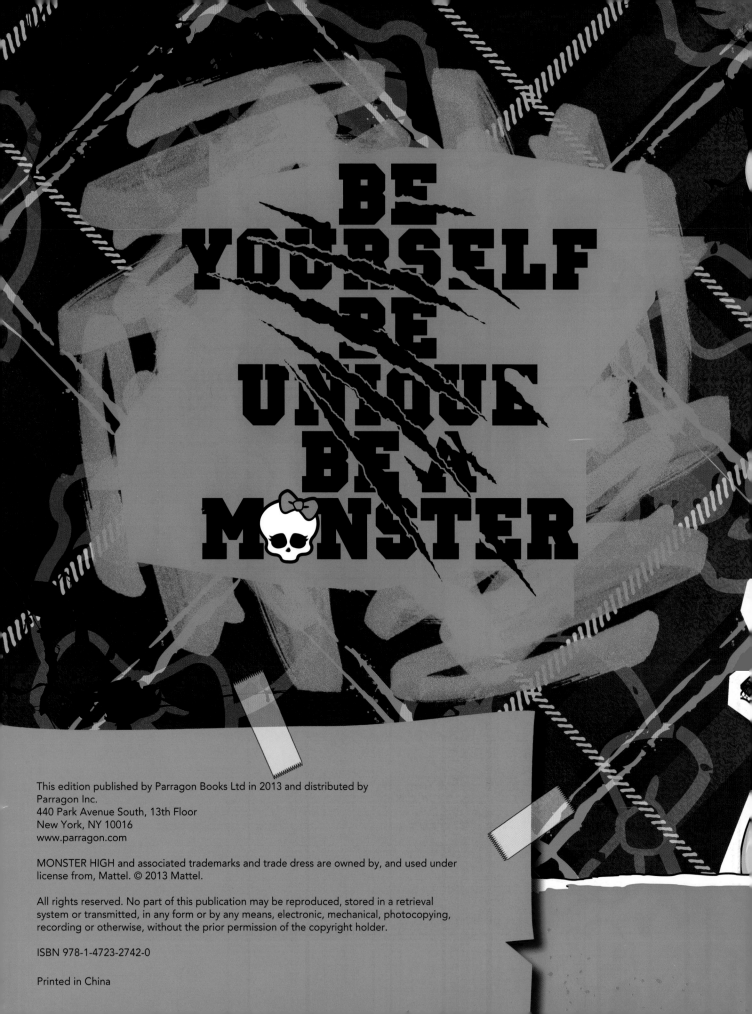

BE YOURSELF BE UNIQUE BE A MONSTER

This edition published by Parragon Books Ltd in 2013 and distributed by
Parragon Inc.
440 Park Avenue South, 13th Floor
New York, NY 10016
www.parragon.com

MONSTER HIGH and associated trademarks and trade dress are owned by, and used under
license from, Mattel. © 2013 Mattel.

ISBN 978-1-4723-2742-0

Printed in China

MONSTER HIGH

fearbook™
class of the century

A monster hello and clawsome congrats on owning a coveted copy of the latest Monster High Fearbook! Our dead-icated team has worked tirelessly through the night to bring you a wicked record of all the comings and ghoulings at the best monster school in town. Inside you'll find student body profiles, monstrous memoirs, and piles of scary-cool pix.

Enjoy. It's gonna be golden!

The Fearbook Team

Xxxxxxxx

PaRragon

Bath · New York · Singapore · Hong Kong · Cologne · Delhi
Melbourne · Amsterdam · Johannesburg · Shenzhen

Frankie Stein™

Draculaura™

Favorite subject:
History

Worst subject:
Swimming—electricity and water don't mix.

GFFs:
Draculaura and Clawdeen Wolf

Extra-scare-icular activities:
Fearleading squad.

I'm never without …
high-voltage hair! My black-and-white streaks are hard to miss.

I'm always saying …
"bolts!"

My ghoulfriends say I'm …
electrifyingly enthusiastic and scarily stylish.

Favorite subject:
Creative writing

Worst subject:
Ge-ogre-phy

GFFs:
Frankie Stein and Clawdeen Wolf

Extra-scare-icular activities:
Fearleading squad;
Newspaper Club President

I'm never without …
Count Fabulous™, my BFF—that's Bat Friend Forever. Oh, and a make-up bag full of "Fierce & Flawless" products.

I'm always saying …
"fangtastic!"

My ghoulfriends say I'm …
the most fiendishly friendly vampire around.

Clawdeen Wolf™

Favorite subject:
Economics—I'm going to set up my own fashion empire.

Worst subject:
Gym (they won't let me wear my platform heels).

GFFs:
Draculaura and Frankie Stein

Extra-scare-icular activities:
Fearleading squad; soccer team; track team; Fashion Entrepreneur Club

I'm never without ...
the latest hot bag or shoes— a ghoul can never have too many clawsome accessories.

I'm always saying ...
"clawsome!"

My ghoulfriends say I'm ...
a fierce fashionista who's loyal to the claw.

Cleo de Nile™

Favorite subject:
Geometry (it involves pyramid shapes).

Worst subject:
History—been there, seen that!

GFFs:
Ghoulia Yelps, and Deuce Gorgon is my boyfriend.

Extra-scare-icular activities:
Captain of the fearleading squad

I'm never without ...
my bag of cursed icons—I never know when I might need them.

I'm always saying ...
"oh my ra!"

My ghoulfriends say I'm ...
the most golden and talented head of Fear Squad ... ever!

7

Lagoona Blue™

Ghoulia Yelps™

Favorite subject:
Oceanography of course!

Worst subject:
Geology

GFFs:
Frankie, Clawdeen, Draculaura, Cleo, Abbey ... I'm a friendly kind of ghoul.

Extra-scare-icular activities:
Swim team captain

I'm never without ...
a tube of monsturizer—I don't want my skin to dry up when I'm out of the water.

I'm always saying ...
"something's fishy!"

My ghoulfriends say I'm ...
a creepy-calm and caring crusader.

Favorite subject:
This is like asking me to choose which one of my zombie relatives I prefer! I love them all equally.

Worst subject:
There is something to be learned from every class. Even dodgeball teaches us to duck.

GFFs:
Cleo de Nile and Spectra Vondergeist

Extra-scare-icular activities:
Comic Book Club president

I'm never without ...
my schedule—it's even synced to my iCoffin!

I'm always saying ...
"uggh ruuur!"

My ghoulfriends say I'm ...
frighteningly smart.

8

Abbey Bominable™

Favorite subject:
Math

Worst subject:
Drama—only kind of scene I like is view of mountains.

GFFs:
Lagoona Blue and Frankie Stein

Extra-scare-icular activities:
Snowboarding team captain

I'm never without ...
my ice crystal necklace—it cools air around me so I am not getting too hot.

I'm always saying ...
"cool it!"

My ghoulfriends say I'm ...
strong and very long—I mean to say tall. And have warm heart under icy touch.

Spectra Vondergeist™

Favorite subject:
Journalism—it runs through the places where my veins used to be.

Worst subject:
Math—it's never open to interpretation.

GFFs:
Ghoulia Yelps

Extra-scare-icular activities:
Newspaper Club (weekly column Oh My Oracle and online blog Ghostly Gossip).

I'm never without ...
my camera and iCoffin—I don't want to miss a monster scoop!

I'm always saying ...
"I've been waiting my entire death to cover a story like this!"

My ghoulfriends say I'm ...
a ghostly gossip guru.

Robecca Steam™

Rochelle Goyle™

Favorite subject:
Metalwork

Worst subject:
Home Ick—although I'm fangtastic
at boiling water!

GFFs:
Rochelle Goyle and Frankie Stein

Extra-scare-icular activities:
Skultimate Roller Maze

I'm never without ...
a set of wrenches and my
rocket boots, which are great
for pulling scary-cool stunts.

I'm always saying ...
"full scream ahead!"

My ghoulfriends say I'm ...
the school scare-devil.

Favorite subject:
Architecture

Worst subject:
Swimming—I sink like stone.

GFFs:
Ghoulia Yelps, Robecca Steam, and
Venus McFlytrap

Extra-scare-icular activities:
Skultimate Roller Maze

I'm never without ...
a book—I've loved reading ever
since my family chose to protect
the Monster High library.

I'm always saying ...
"travel beyond the stone you sit on."

My ghoulfriends say I'm ...
horribly hardheaded and
dead-fully protective.

10

Venus McFlytrap™

Favorite subject:
Biteology

Worst subject:
Woodwork—I can hear the screams when the saw cuts.

GFFs:
Lagoona, Robecca, Rochelle, Frankie, and Ghoulia.

Extra-scare-icular activities:
Chairmonster of the Monster High Green Party

I'm never without ...
my pollens of persuasion—they have a funny effect on those around me.

I'm always saying ...
"don't be a loser, be a re-user!"

My ghoulfriends say I'm ...
a loveable tree-hugger who leads by example.

Deuce Gorgon™

Favorite subject:
Home Ick—it's the best class at Monster High.

Worst subject:
Home Ick—I pretend to hate it!

GFFs:
Jackson Jekyll is my beast bud, and Cleo de Nile is my ughsome ghoulfriend.

Extra-scare-icular activities:
Casketball team (guard)

I'm never without ...
my shades—otherwise it's a rockin' day at Monster High, you get me?

I'm always saying ...
"hey monster, what's up?"

My friends say I'm ...
a scary-cool skater dude with attitude.

Favorite subject: Biteology—my long-term scareer goal is to work in sports medicine.
Worst subject: Home Ick
GFFs: A pack leader never has favorites!

Extra-scare-icular activities: Football team captain
My friends say I'm ... furrociously athletic and surprisingly smart.

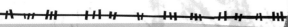
Clawd Wolf™

Favorite subject: Music history—music is my un-life.
Worst subject: Mad Science. Sorry Mr. Hack, the only thing I wanna create is scary-sweet music!
GFFs: Deuce Gorgon and Holt Hyde

Extra-scare-icular activities: Monster High Music Society member
My ghoulfriends say I'm ... the ghoul with the un-earthly voice and va-va-voom vintage style.

Operetta™

Favorite subject: Mad Science—guess it's in my blood.
Worst subject: Physical deaducation, especially when we play dodgeball!
GFFs: Frankie Stein and Deuce Gorgon

Extra-scare-icular activities: Monster High Music Society member
My friends say I'm ... crazy-cool (for a normie), although scarily unreliable at times.

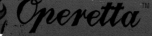
Jackson Jekyll™

Favorite subject: Music theory—you don't get to be the beast DJ around by luck!
Worst subject: Everything else

GFFs: I'm down with any monster who digs my beats.
Extra-scare-icular activities: Skultimate Roller Maze player
My friends say I'm ... a smokin' hot mixer.

Holt Hyde™

Favorite subject:
Psychology—understanding humans is vital to giving advice.
Worst subject:
Clawculus—equations don't solve every problem.

GFFs: I adore monsters like Draculaura who are in love with love.
Extra-scare-icular activities: Daily radio show from my studio in the catacombs.
My ghoulfriends say I'm ... frighteningly frilly and wickedly wise.

C.A. Cupid ™

Favorite subject: Drama—I can mimic other monsters purrfectly.
Worst subject: Anything which gets my purrfect paws dirty.
GFFs: Meowlody and Purrsephone

Extra-scare-icular activities: Debate team member—I adore a good argument.
My ghoulfriends say I'm ... a catty kitty who never comes when I'm called.

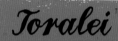 *Toralei* ™

Favorite subject: Mad Science—especially the module on genetics.
Worst subject: Home Ick—Ms. Kindergrübber makes us wear full-body hairnets.

GFFs: Meowlody and Toralei
Extra-scare-icular activities: Gymnastics Club—we always land on our feet.
My ghoulfriends say I'm ... purrfectly identical to my sister.

Purrsephone ™

Favorite subject: Mad Science—especially the module on genetics.
Worst subject: Home Ick—Ms. Kindergrübber makes us wear full-body hairnets.

GFFs: Purrsephone and Toralei
Extra-scare-icular activities: Gymnastics Club—we always land on our feet.
My ghoulfriends say I'm ... purrfectly identical to my sister.

 *Meowlody* ™

Favorite subject: Literature—I love to lose myself in books.
Worst subject: Any class where Mr. Zarr is booked as the substitute creature.

GFFs: HooDude Voodoo
Extra-scare-icular activities: Growl Choir member
My ghoulfriends say I'm ... friendly and wail-y helpful.

Scarah Screams™

Favorite subject: Swimming
Worst subject: Mad Science—except when Lagoona and I get paired up for assignments!

GFFs: Deuce Gorgon and Lagoona Blue
Extra-scare-icular activities: Swim Team member
My friends say I'm ... laid-back and sensitive, but an unbeatable monster in the pool!

Gillington "Gil" Webber™

Favorite subject: Music—I'm an avid guitar player.
Worst subject: Any class when I don't get to sit next to a scary-cute ghoul.

GFFs: Clawd Wolf, Deuce Gorgon, Gil Webber
Extra-scare-icular activities: Track team
My friends say I'm ... the fire and soul of the party!

Heath Burns™

Favorite subject: Physical deaducation
Worst subject: Music—I can't stand Heath Burns' guitar playing.

GFFs: Gil Webber, Heath Burns. I have a crush on Ghoulia Yelps.
Extra-scare-icular activities: Chess Club member, casketball team member
My friends say I'm ... deathly slow, but sorta sweet.

Sloman "Slo Mo" Mortavitch™

Favorite subject: Scarecology —I'd like to counsel other monsters.

Worst subject: Volcanology— unsurprising seeing as I'm made of cloth. I'm not a fan of subjects involving fire!

GFFs: Scarah Screams, Frankie Stein

Extra-scare-icular activities: Football team— I'm the tackling target.

My friends say I'm ... a grrrreat listener who can be a horrific pain—due to my voodoo flaw.

HooDude Voodoo ™

We don't want to miss any student from the Monster High Fearbook! Use the space below to add your photo and details.

Favorite subject: ....

Worst subject: ....

GFFs: ....

....

Extra-scare-icular activities: ....

....

My ghoulfriends say I'm ... .

....

The most UGH-MAZING events of the year!

It's been another fangtastic year at Monster High. Here are just some of the ugh-mazing events that have shocked our world....

WE'VE GOT SPIRITS HOW BOUT YOU?

Cleo's kicking party

Yes, we know it wasn't strictly in school time, but Cleo de Nile's end-of-term party was the hottest ticket this year! The event showcased the talents of new student body Holt Hyde, who set the decks on fire with a succession of monster mixes and hot hits.

Claws out at the Shaky-spear clawditions

Monster High has a long tradition of paw-formance art, and this year's show was the beast yet! Draculaura starred as Awf-elia in *Hamlet The Musical*, but competition was fierce for the lead role. As a result, two of the school's most exceptionally talon-ted student bodies were notable by their absence. Cleo de Nile and Clawdeen Wolf were so dead-termined to upstage each other, they ended up getting injured.

Fangs a million Frankie!

All eyes were on Frankie Stein when she scooped first prize in a scary-cool video competition on KBLOOD Radio. She won an impromptu gig from the Jaundice Brothers—the most gruesome group on the planet!
The school went crazy when the guys dropped in to play live at the Homecarnage concert.

Spirits lift at the Spirit Rally

A grrreat turn-out at this year's Spirit Rally ensured that thousands were raised for the school football team. Appearances by swim and casketball team captains Lagoona Blue and Clawd Wolf got the party started, while a star performance from Cleo's Fear Squad ensured the night went with a fang!

SPOOKTACULAR SPORTS

These pages are dead-icated to our fangtastic Fear Squad led by golden ghoul Cleo de Nile. Here we chart the team's progress to Monster Mashional success.

1

2

Frankie Stein injected new blood into this year's Fear Squad ...

4

Practice made almost paw-fect.....

3

... but under Cleo's tough tutelage the new line-up didn't last.

5

Failure to be selected for Gloom Beach left Cleo devastated.

7

The Fear Squad launched a campaign to get there on a wild card.....

6

All they had to do was make a video that scored at least 10 million views online. Bolts!

Luckily Ghoulia's computer skills saved the day ...

8

... the Monster High Fear Squad was off to Gloom Beach!

10

After a week of hard work with Scary Murphy, the team won the coveted Spirit Staff ...

11

... but new coach Nefera created chaos by firing the team and bringing in new recruits!

NEWS FLASH

16

12

13

Cleo's dedicated Team B Fear Squad couldn't be stopped ...

14

... even by Nefera. They won the Mashionals!

15

Congrats to the runners up— Monster High Team A.

On a somber note, Nefera de Nile was stripped of her four previous Mashional titles due to un-sports-monster-like behavior.

19

SPOOKTACULAR SPORTS

GORY CASKETBALL GLORY

Clawd Wolf led the Monster High casketball team to great frights this year, beating Smogsnorts Vampyr Academy and Crescent Moon High to championship triumph. Clawd seems set for a casketball college scholarship for sure.

Sadly, Deuce Gorgon has been out for much of the season after spraining a snake.

SCARY-FAST SWIMMERS

Saltwater sweetie Lagoona Blue has led by example in the pool this year. She and freshwater team-mate Gillington Webber finished top of the league! The Monster High swimmers snatched the trophy from Belfry Prep.

FUR-IOUS TRACK ACTION

Some of the most eek-citing rivalry on the track recently has come from within the school. Heath Burns, sizzling star for the guys' team, was put in his place by the ghouls' talon-ted captain, Clawdeen Wolf. The challenge began when Heath threw down the gauntlet, claiming that ghouls were too delicate for the track. The answer from Clawdeen? "I got more hustle in one claw than you've got in your whole body!"

Sadly, Heath had forgotten that a full moon puts Clawdeen in a furrocious frenzy. The wolf stormed to an easy victory.

INSPIRING HOWL

"At first I wasn't sure that I could make the track meet because my little brother bit my leg, but I refused to let it stop me. I had to win!"

Clawdeen X

21

Abyss friends forever

The beast thing about un-life at school is the monsters. I have the best ghoulfriends in the whole world and know they will always go that extra mile for me—or swim that extra fathom! That's what happened when Frankie asked to borrow the scary-gorgeous necklace that Clawd had given me. Of course I said yes right away. We love swapping outfits, and I had borrowed a pair of her killer heels only the week before!

As Frankie put the necklace on, she accidentally touched both her bolts. The shock sent the bling flying into … the deep end of the pool! Frankie is such a newbie, I had to explain to her that no one goes in the deep end, EVER! The pool is the deepest in the world—no one knows what lurks at the bottom.

Frankie, being Frankie, insisted on climbing into a deep-sea diving suit. Before I could say "blundering bats" she was in the pool with Lagoona, who's like the best swimmer in the whole of Monster High! The ghouls dodged lots of scary creatures down there, before finding my necklace in a cave guarded by a giant squid. The naughty beast was hoarding a whole stack of other treasures that had fallen in the water over the years. Frankie shocked the squid into returning everything—from my necklace to Jackson's favorite T97X4 clawculator. My fearsome friends did the whole school a favor that day!

Draculaura

NO SUBSTITUTE FOR GOOD LISTENING

Some teachers at Monster High are pretty ughsome! I personally kinda like Ms. Kindergrübber, though I'd never admit in public that my favorite class is Home Ick.

Anyhow, among all the brilliantly talon-ted faculty members there is one horrible exception—Mr. Lou Zarr, the substitute creature. I imagine the first time we met will stick with him forever. I came in late to class (which, granted, is pretty annoying) but it couldn't be avoided cause I was totally getting changed after casketball practice. Mr. Zarr got razzed. I don't think it helped after he said, "You're late," and I replied, "Nah, I'm Deuce, Deuce Gorgon!" He then told me to take off my shades. Baaaad move, so, so bad!

I tried to tell Mr. Zarr, but he wouldn't listen. Even when all the other monsters in class covered their faces with books, he didn't get it. So I took my glasses off and ... whaddya know? There was a new statue at Monster High. Loser in stone! What? Oh sorry, make that "Lou Zarr" in stone!

DEUCE

CLUBS

Fashion Entrepreneurs Club

The main event in the club's calendar was the Fashion Talon Show, part of the 1,361st annual Fashion Show. The event was a howling success due to the jaw-dropping performance of founding member Clawdeen Wolf. The fierce fashionista put on a catwalk show to make flesh crawl and fur stand on end, strutting her stuff in her own designs like a true professional. It's not known what caused the changes to Clawdeen's routine, but the spotlights in the room may have replicated the effect of a full moon.

1361st ANNUAL CHARITY FASHION SHOW

24

NEWSPAPER CLUB

Monster High's Newspaper Club has benefited from the hard work and enthusiasm of two particular members this year. Budding photographer Draculaura has captured some of the school's standout moments on camera for the front page. The gossip section has also been dripping with ghoulish details thanks to journalist-in-the-making Spectra Vondergeist. Next year the club is looking forward to fostering a closer working partnership with the school's catacomb-based radio-station presenter C.A. Cupid. It's all part of the team's bid to make Monster High a multimedia zone.

DEBATE TEAM

Mr. Where's Debate Team has enjoyed a howlingly fulfilled year at the rostrum. Subjects up for debate have included "Monsters and the wider world" and "To devour or not to devour?" The team welcomed new member Venus McFlytrap who has a particular interest in ecological matters. Miss McFlytrap is eager for her voice to be heard.

CLUBS

Comic Book Club

Comic Book Club president, Ghoulia Yelps, is as dead-icated a collector as she is an illustrator. This year, the school even enjoyed an exhibition of some of her work! Her personal highlight was the surprising acquisition of the ultra-rare first edition of the *DeadFast* comic. The precious mag was given to her by an unlikely and extremely generous benefactor.

DEADFAST
#0

FIRST ISSUE

Woosh!

OMG!

Ghoulia sketching her comic book hero.

CHESS CLUB

Chess has proven the perfect hobby for Sloman "Slo Mo" Mortavitch. The lumbering zombie is blazing a trail through both intra- and inter-school competitions. Zombies excel at chess, due to the pace of the game and the logic required. Fellow club member and Slo Mo appreciator Ghoulia Yelps, writes, "We fully expect him to achieve Growl Master status."

GO SLO MO!

Growl Choir

It has been a time of consolidation and hard work for the choir as they attempt to make the grade for next year's Growl Choir Of The Year contest. There was, however, a major set back mid term when the choirmaster got sucked through a broken window during practice. The window pane shattered when Cleo de Nile's scream reverberated around the school after her squad's initial rejection from the Gloom Beach Fearleading Championships. Luckily, the master has since made an almost full recovery and can now see through both eyes again.

Terrifying TRIPS

Monte Carlo

ALL SET FOR MONTE CARLO

What goes on tour, scares on tour! Let's go out and about with the Monster High student bodies....

FRANKIE SNEEZED FIRST

CLAWDEEN GOT SICK, TOO

Budget issues meant that the proposed visit to Scaris was cancelled, but the fangtastic Monte Carlo trip did go ahead as planned, despite an uncertain beginning. Prior to departure, Frankie Stein came down with a hideous virus, with Clawdeen, Draculaura, and Cleo de Nile all getting infected. Luckily, the trip was saved by exchange student Abbey Bominable! The bold ghoul braved the catacombs to find the antidote, monster thistle, despite being allergic herself. It's just another example of how fiendishly friendly student bodies can be!

EVEN DRACULAURA AND CLEO BROKE OUT IN SPOTS!

WITHOUT ABBEY, THE TRIP WOULD HAVE BEEN A DEAD LOSS

Mad Science Fair

THE FAIR

Student bodies from Monster High enjoyed an educational day out of class at the school's Mad Science Fair. Amid the many, many entries from monstrous schools up and down the country, Cleo de Nile's amazing project stood out. Her machine to turn trash into green fuel bagged her first prize from Headmistress Bloodgood.

ANOTHER INTERESTING ENTRY

Gloom Beach

READY TO GO

HEATH BURNS SUPPLIED
THE TUNES

THE BUS

SOME RARE TIME OFF
FOR THE FEAR SQUAD

THE GANG PLAY
WATER POLO

SPIRIT STAFF FOR
MONSTER HIGH

Spirits were high on the bus to Gloom Beach this year—despite Heath Burns' non-stop guitar playing! The student bodies couldn't wait to let their fur down and soak up the spring sun.

The trip promised more work than play for Monster High's Fear Squad. The ghouls were based on the South Beach in order to take part in a fearleading camp and competition. Scary Murphy put the squad through their paces every single day. The hard work paid off—the ghouls brought the winners' Spirit Staff back to Monster High!

THE WINNING
ASSIGNMENT

CLEO'S
~~GHOULIA'S~~ PROJECT

CLEO GETS
THE TROPHY

monstrous

MEMORIES

What's your favorite Monster High moment? Here's a collection of our most cherished paw-sonal memories....

"Where to start? I have been solely responsible for so many ugh-mazing moments this year. Getting us invited to Gloom Beach, winning the Spirit Staff, triumphing at the Mashionals! Oh and sticking it to Nefera, sister of doom!" Cleo

"Rewiring HooDude's brain to give him more confidence. You don't get to do that often!" Scarah

"It was pretty incredible working with Frankie on our life-sized gingerbread guy for Home Ick. Doing anything with Frankie is ugh-mazing!" Jackson Jekyll

"I enjoyed the power outage caused by Heath Burns which meant that all technology died at Monster High! For one day I got to show the student bodies how they could exist without their iCoffins, tablets and clawculators!" Robecca

"I loved working with that fine monster Deuce on a track for his ungrateful ghoulfriend. The chance to write for someone who appreciates my little ol' style of music cancelled out the stress of dealin' with that total pain, Cleo." Operetta

"When Frankie got everyone—including me—tickets to see Jason Biter in concert! She's the beast GFF ever!" Ghoulia

"I remember when the ghouls tried to make me feeling not so much home sick by locking me into freezer. Was very kindness to me. Almost making me to cry." Abbey

"My favorite memory was when the ghouls dressed Slo Mo up as my aunt to attend the Parent-Creature Conference. He looked bonzer! There were no worries anyhow because the teacher just wanted to talk about my excellent grades!" Lagoona

"WATCHING JACKSON JEKYLL CHANGE INTO HOLT HYDE FOR THE FIRST TIME. HILARIOUS! AND GETTING A DATE WITH DRACULAURA, YEAH, THOSE ARE MY TWO TOP MEMORIES THIS YEAR." Heath

"I'll never forget the look on those werecats' faces when they got sent to trigular calcometry summer camp—with a stink bomb on board the bus!" Ghoulia

"It was totes amazing when our GFFs planned a surprise joint party for Draculaura and me. It was my Sweet 16 days and her Sweet 1,600 years! We had both been trying to sort out a party for each other, but no one could come, because they were all planning a joint party for us both!" Frankie

"Uuuughghghghhuughhg!"

(Ghoulia led our zombie team to victory at Dodgeball by using her trigular calcometry skills.) Slo Mo

"I loved it when Emily Anne came to school for Monster High's "We Stop Hate" campaign. She spread so much love, love, love!" Draculaura

"WHEN THE ZOMBIES WERE FIGHTING OVER GHOULIA YELPS! I'VE SEEN PAINT DRY FASTER!" Holt Hyde

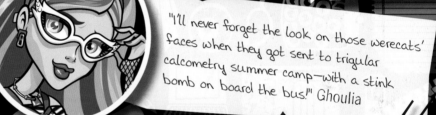

FEARSOME FACULTY

We at Monster High are privileged to have a deadly team of academics helping to fill our skulls with knowledge. These pages are dead-icated to our fearsome faculty members.

Carbon | Rhenium | Platinum | Arsenic | Technetium | Vampirium

Headless Headmistress Bloodgood
Headmistress and Trigular Calcometry 101 Teacher

Credentials:

Sleepy Hollow State B.S. Equestrian Studies
Marie Antoinette AEM M.A. Horticulture/Para-Psychology

Common Bloodgood-isms....

"Tallyho Nightmare ... away!"

"Losing your head is no excuse for not doing the right thing!"

Why we love her....

"Because she is letting me stay while I am doing my studies at the school and am being so very far away from home in the mountains. I think she is good lady."

Abbey Bominable

"She is very nice with animals, which is important for our world." Venus McFlytrap

"Because she is a great and inspirational role model to the student bodies."

Ghoulia Yelps

Best Bloodgood moments

"When she let me and the girls have an overnight creepover in the school on Frightday the 13th! I got to make Toralei eat furballs 'cause we made it through the night without getting spooked by the beast of coffin corridor. We threw him a totally ughsome party!"
Cleo de Nile

"When she chained me and Abbey together for the day to teach us to get along. It turned out to be a voltageous idea and now we're beast friends."
Frankie Stein

Ms. Kindergrübber
Home Ick Teacher

Mr. Hackington
Mad Science Teacher

Credentials:

Skinner College – B.S. Chemistry
Lancet and Czechit School of Science
– M.S. Taxidermy

Why we love him....

"Despite the fact that he loves to cut things up in his class, like poor little frogs—which is never cool—he's not afraid to back down under pressure from sea creatures." Lagoona Blue

Best 'Hack' moments

"When, like, he turned up with some blood sausages during casketball—that meaty snack helped me win the game!"
Clawd Wolf

"When his 'care for an egg' assignment went horrifically wrong. The egg hatched and attacked Mr. H!"
Gil Webber

Common Hack-isms....

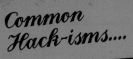

"HEATH BURNS!!!!! Do you want to end up in deadtention for the rest of your life?"

Mr. D'eath
Student Guidance Counselor

Best Mr. D'eath moments

"He let me give him a monster makeover and set him up on a date. Now that's scary-cool!"
Rochelle Goyle

"HE SIGHS A LOT— BUT HE'S ONE FANGTASTICALLY HAPPY DUDE."
Deuce Gorgon

Common D'eath-isms....

"What's the worst that could happen?"

Credentials:

North Styx State B.A. Modern Dance/Journalism
Tombstone Tech M.A. Peace Studies

Why we love him....

"Because he's a little freaky just like us. He's got this 'regret list' where he writes down all the things he plans on regretting before the death of his soul." Frankie Stein

Credentials:

GGT Ghoul Graduate Trainee—retrained after formerly running "cottage" baking industry and then running a B&B.

Why we love her....

"Because, for some reason she quite likes me—we kinda bond over my stitching." Frankie Stein

"That smells spooktacular Deuce! The rest of you ... back to the chopping board."

Common Grübbisms....

Best Kindergrübber moment

"WhΣn mΣ and FrankiΣ madΣ a living gingΣrbrΣad man in hΣr class. ShΣ lovΣd thΣ big guy!"
Jackson Jekyll

Horrors of High School

NEED A SHRINK?

I always find it ugh-mazing that students whose brains are still half empty —like caverns full of cobwebs—think they know everything! How do they expect to fool experienced teachers such as I, Mr. Hackington?

During one Mad Science class, I was called away to deal with a dragon. I told the students to sit still and not touch the powerful and dangerous piece of technology on my desk. Of course no sooner was I out of the room than Master Burns began to fiddle! With a flick of a switch, every student body was shrunk to the size of an ant.

Abbey Bominable, a clever and focused ghoul, realized there must be a "reverse" switch on the machine, but the students were too small to get to it. Flashy Burns thought he could fix things by making a paper plane and flying over to my desk. What he didn't factor in was crashing to the ground after his flaming hair set the plane on fire. All seemed lost. The class were certain I would return, find out what had happened and they would all be doomed!

Luckily, Abbey used her head. Clawd squirted liquid from a syringe toward my desk, then Abbey used her powers to freeze it into an ice bridge. The pair reached the machine and flicked the "reverse" switch.

By the time I walked into the room everyone sat in their seats as if nothing had happened. The class still spent a week in deadtention however. Why? Because they had also managed to enlarge a spider that had been scuttling across my desk at the time. The giant arachnid gave the students away! (I made sure that it, too, got a deadtention.)

Mr. Hackington

TECH NO FEAR!

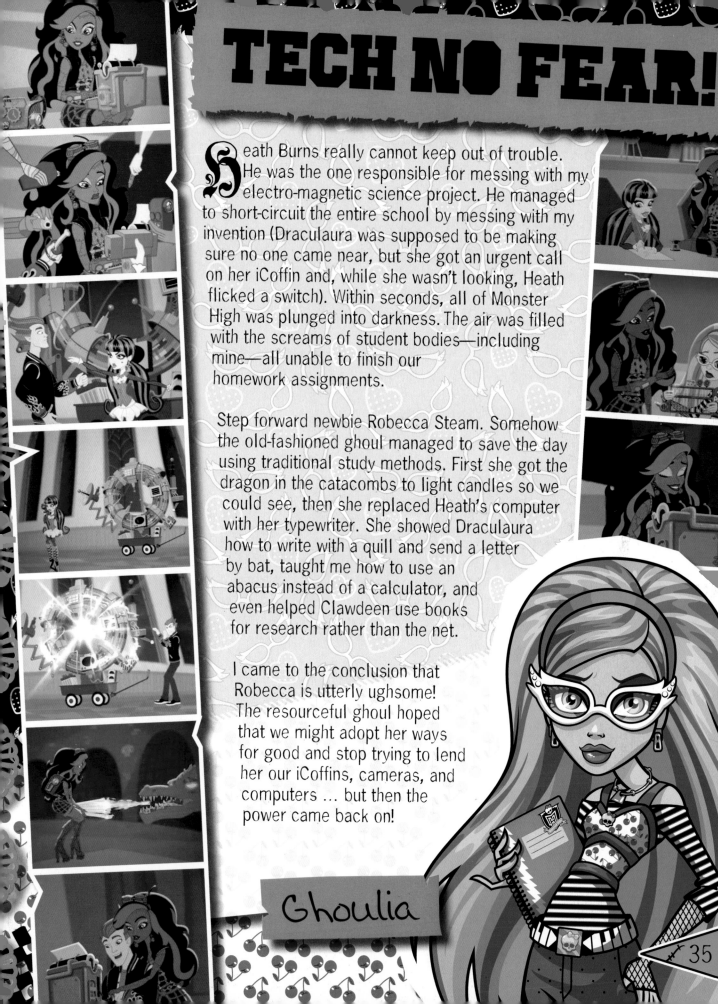

Heath Burns really cannot keep out of trouble. He was the one responsible for messing with my electro-magnetic science project. He managed to short-circuit the entire school by messing with my invention (Draculaura was supposed to be making sure no one came near, but she got an urgent call on her iCoffin and, while she wasn't looking, Heath flicked a switch). Within seconds, all of Monster High was plunged into darkness. The air was filled with the screams of student bodies—including mine—all unable to finish our homework assignments.

Step forward newbie Robecca Steam. Somehow the old-fashioned ghoul managed to save the day using traditional study methods. First she got the dragon in the catacombs to light candles so we could see, then she replaced Heath's computer with her typewriter. She showed Draculaura how to write with a quill and send a letter by bat, taught me how to use an abacus instead of a calculator, and even helped Clawdeen use books for research rather than the net.

I came to the conclusion that Robecca is utterly ughsome! The resourceful ghoul hoped that we might adopt her ways for good and stop trying to lend her our iCoffins, cameras, and computers ... but then the power came back on!

Ghoulia

35

THE GHOSTLY GOSSIP

Wooooooooooo, what a Spectra-cular year it's been for scandal at Monster High! No one (cough) knows the identity of the writer of the fang-scinating Ghostly Gossip blog, but she (cough, or he) certainly has her (or of course, his) ghoulish finger on the flat-lining pulse of the school. Here's a round up of the juiciest news this year.

Heath, HooDude, Jackson, Holt..... Who can keep up with Frankie Stein dating schedule?

Draculaura's love life has been the stuff of nightmares....

A date with a statue? Desperate, much?

Heath managed to woo Draculaura ...

... but when Burns started to "char," Clawd stepped in.

The result? Total friction between Draculaura and Clawd's sister, Clawdeen!

Even golden couple Cleo and Deuce have had their issues!

It's forbidden underwater love for Lagoona and Gil.

Brainiac Ghoulia's love story was a slow-burner.

favorite fang-outs

Ghouls love to fang out together!
Check out our spooktacular top spots.

The Maul

Where to start in the Maul? So many stores, so little time! We love to shop til we drop for scary-cool accessories, and snap up drop-dead gorgeous pieces from our favorite shops to make sure we always have totally unique and killer style!

The creepateria

OK, so the food is mostly gruesome, but the creepateria is definitely the destination of choice for first dates, showdowns, and chats with the ghouls.

Coffin corridor

Whether we're reading the latest copy of *Monster Beat*, swapping beauty tips or discussing hot dates, the coffin corridor is a great place to fang out. It's totes ugh-mazing what we can fit in those coffin-shaped lockers—bags full of sugared eyeballs, Fierce & Flawless products, cursed idols, plus the odd frog or twenty!

Cleo's golden boudoir

Oh My Ra! Cleo's bedroom is scarily spacious. We love hanging here and playing the board game *Gargoyles to Gargoyles*—although everyone except Abbey lets Cleo win.

The Coffin Bean

The drinks are to die for at the Coffin Bean—they're poured by the monster world's beast barista, Lagoona Blue! We head here to rest our weary, high-heeled paws after a hard night's shopping.

The Juicer

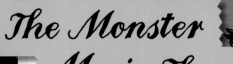

When we can't get off the school grounds to go to the Maul, the juicer is the next best thing! Just make sure you don't go with Abbey—unless you want a smoothie frozen so hard it'll crack your fangs!

Clawdeen's clawsome cave

Clawdeen's crib is as fierce as you'd expect a werewolf's room to be. The purple color scheme and animal print furnishings scream glamour. Her closet is so packed with ughsome outfits, her sister Howleen can't keep away!

The Monster Movie Theater

Deuce loves scary human movies, Clawd's into action, while silent movies are more Jackson's scream. Whatever the guys wanna watch is fine with us ... as long as it involves popcorn in the dark!

Draculaura's dark den

Draculaura's room is pink, black and totes adorable—just like its owner. We head there after school when we want to pamp with the vamp!

Frankie's fab lab

Frankie sleeps in the basement laboratory she calls "the fab". It's pretty unique as bedrooms go—dark, forbidding, and stacked full of crazy machines and electrical wiring—perfect for spooky creepovers.

EEK!

They're the embarrassing photos they didn't want you to see. Be prepared to laugh yourself into an early grave with these Monster High howlers!

back in your coffin

Ready for our close-ups after a workout with Coach Igor.

Cleo discovers Frankie's freaky flaw.

Eeek scary makeover, Draculaura!

Soak it up, Heath!

Gargoyle attacks the Hack.

Hope you're wearing your Freaky & Fabulous waterproof mascara, Cleo!

Deuce gets a taste of his own "stone" medicine.

40

Ribbit!

Lightning strike!

Bolts! Frankie reversed her polarity!

Want a steakout, Draculaura?

Scary hair day, Cleo?

Back off!

Going for a dip, kitties?

Glacial facial! Heath gets a frosty reception from Abbey.

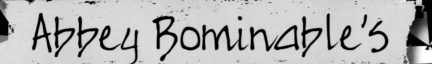

Abbey Bominable's
QUOTES OF THE YEAR

Unlike we mountain-dwelling monsters who are not into the small talk, the Monster High student bodies love to be doing chat together. Here are some of the best sound bites I have heard when fanging out in the howlways.

"I didn't have time to study. I got busy. You think these pores just shrink themselves?"
Draculaura

"Knowledge is the cure for every curse."
Mr. Hack

"YOU LOOK HORRIBLE! I LIKE THAT IN a GiRL!"
Heath

"No way am I going out with a guy with more than four eyes ... and he has like, eight!" Frankie

"I nailed the finals like a coffin, sista!"
Clawdeen

"Woah! Slow ya growls."
Clawd

"Holt Hyde? No, I don't know him."
Jackson

"Draculaura, you're pretty pumped for somebody without a pulse!" Cleo

"WHO YOU CALLIN' A BULL?" Manny

44

"Cleo's been working that cursed idol like a credit card with no limit!" Clawdeen

"MONSTER HIGH'S ABOUT BEING COOL TO EVERYONE NO MATTER WHO OR WHAT YOU ARE, EVEN IF THAT MEANS A 'NORMIE'." Deuce

"It might come back to bite ya!" Lagoona

"If I don't get a scoop soon, I'm just gonna live!" Spectra

"I don't mind when people talk about me, it's when they stop talking about you that you have to worry." Nefera

"I couldn't study for the SAT, my brother ate all my notes." Clawdeen

"I just want to crawl into a puddle and pull it over the top of me!" Lagoona

"She does so much for me I thought I should do something nice for her—but don't tell anyone, it'll totally ruin my rep." Cleo

"Let's just say my clothes aren't the only thing that's fierce during a full moon!" Clawdeen

"I've known Clawd since before he was housebroken." Draculaura

"Y'all are pickin' on the wrong fiddle." Operetta

"UuuughrrrghghghUgh." Ghoulia

"No one is to look directly at me unless it's in amazement." Cleo

"I DON'T GIVE A'S!" Mr. Rotter

"You are one misdeed away from the study howl of eternal homework—oh, and fiery demons will descend upon your house." Headmistress Bloodgood

"Voltageous fail! It was like I had death breath." Frankie

"DO YOU BELIEVE IN LOVE AT FIRST FRIGHT? OR SHOULD I WALK BY AGAIN...?" Heath

We find out who runs things and we show them who's boss. Then we ghouls will run the school." Toralei

45

Horrors of High School

Truth or scare

I've only just joined Monster High, but everyone here is fiendishly friendly. I can't wait to be invited to one of the ghoul's famous slumber parties. The last one sounded scary-cool!

On the night of the party, all of the ghouls rocked up to Clawdeen's lair to fang out and chat. Frankie was totes freaked after reading in *Monster Beat* magazine about the game "truth or scare" where GFFs choose either a dare or to tell a shocking secret.

Frankie didn't like the idea of telling Cleo the truth about which boy she was crushing on, so she tried a lot of stalling tactics to avoid playing the game. But crafty Cleo wouldn't let it drop. She scared Frankie to send a text to all the boys at Monster High saying, "Party at my house—spread the word".

Cleo couldn't believe it when Frankie actually plucked up the courage to send the text. "Your parents are going to freak when all those boys turn up at your house!" she cackled.

The joke was on Cleo when she discovered that Frankie had sent the text from *her* iCoffin! The boys were stampeding over to Cleo's as they spoke! Spookily enough, that was the last time Miss de Nile suggested a game of truth or scare!

Rochelle

Lagoona's Aunt Lantic

My ghoulfriend Lagoona's a straight A student. If only my parents would meet her they'd discover how bright and intelligent she is, sigh!

Being super-smart, Lagoona freaked out when one of her teachers asked to see her parents to discuss her work. She just couldn't understand it! The sitch got worse when Clawdeen told her that she must have totally failed. My poor salty was beside her fins with anxiety!

That's when Clawdeen came up with possibly her most bizarre idea ever. She suggested dressing someone up as one of Lagoona's family so her folks wouldn't find out that she'd failed. The question was who? Slo Mo happened to be slouching nearby. Before he could say "uuugggrrhh!", he was being made up to look like Lagoona's fake "Aunt Lantic".

Slo Mo looked truly ugh-ful, but he went in to see the teacher anyway. Everyone waited on tenter-claws outside. Luckily the plan ran like a nightmare. Not only was the teacher fooled, he also explained that he wanted to see Lagoona's folks to tell them that she'd written her best ever essay.

I was so proud of Lagoona. Now I just have to convince my folks that she's the best thing since sliced pondweed!

Gil

Dear lowly students of Monster High,

As you come to the end of another year you may be pondering your future, wondering how you will make your freakily unique way in the world when you leave Monster High. I, Nefera de Nile, high-flying and popular former student of this very school had the same fears before I graduated.

Luckily, I soon discovered that my time here was a stepping-stone to greater things. I am now a famous supermodel, gracing the catwalks of Europe and earning more gold ingots than I could ever fit in daddy's crypt. The things I learned in classes, like dead languages, have come in handy for demanding the things I need as I jet around the globe.

Of course, none of you can possibly hope to attain the heady heights which I, Nefera, first and best beloved daughter of Ramses, has gained in un-life, but I am sure you will each manage to make your monstrous mark, when and if you graduate.

Yours ugh-mazingly,
Nefera de Nile

P.S. If you see me in the Maul, never speak to me unless you are spoken to.

My favorite memories from this year:

Being brought back as fearleading coach by Headmistress Bloodgood in an attempt to help my little sister's frankly horrific Fear Squad shape up for the Mashionals.

When my little sister Cleo shopped til she dropped at the Maul to get me the latest scary-cool fashions (ok so I was blackmailing her over the party she wanted to throw, but still....)

oh.my.ra!

Do you have to get your evil claws into everything Nefera? I cannot believe you have a page in my Fearbook! What are you even doing in the editor's office anyway? You're not having the last growl this time....

NEFERA KICKED OUT!

HERE ARE SOME REALLY FANGTASTIC PICS OF NEFERA EVERYONE!

This is when we discovered the real reason you'd come back to school—you'd been kicked out of Fashion Week for your monstrous attitude. Your modeling scareer is an epic fail!

And, this is when we fooled you into thinking that toilet paper rolls and garbage cans were the latest look! It certainly was killer style—it totally killed your street cred at the Maul. Ha!

Most likely to....

The students have been voting on the scary-cool stuff we think our GFFs might get up to in the future. Whaddya think? Remember to complete your own 'Most Likely' section too—or ask your school GFFs to do it for you!

Cleo de Nile

Most likely to ... be an A-list star of stage and scream.

Frankie Stein

Most likely to ... help a ghoulfriend in need.

Draculaura

Most likely to ... fly off into the sunset with the monster of her screams.

Clawdeen Wolf

Most likely to ... design the purrfect pair of killer heels.

Ghoulia Yelps

Most likely to ... be the next spookily smart headmistress of Monster High.

Lagoona Blue

Most likely to ... save the wait, whale. Oh bolts!

Most likely to....

Rochelle Goyle

Most likely to ... go on a fangtastic round-the-world trip.

Robecca Steam

Most likely to ... become a Skultimate Roller Maze commentator.

Abbey Bominable

Most likely to ... scale the highest peak of the Severed Andes mountain range.

Spectra Vondergeist

Most likely to ... get her own scary-cool talk show.

Venus McFlytrap

Most likely to ... start a recycling revolution!

Deuce Gorgon

Most likely to ... play the lead in a scary human movie.

Most likely to....

Clawd Wolf

Most likely to ... be chased by a mob of angry villagers.

Jackson Jekyll

Most likely to ... win the No Bells Prize for Mad Science.

Holt Hyde

Most likely to ... make the Monster Top 10 with the "After Midnight" remix of a Jason Biter track.

Operetta

Most likely to ... cause a mass freak out when singing the Monster Mashional anthem at the start of the Fearleading Mashionals.

SCREAM TEAM

Toralei

Most likely to ... become a catty impressionist with a fearsome line in put-downs.

Meowlody and Purrsephone

Most likely to ... prowl off on their own.

Most likely to....

Scarah Screams

Most likely to ... float onto HooDude's couch!

Gillington Webber

Most likely to ... live with his parents until he's 1,000 years old.

Heath Burns

Most likely to ... ask Nefera de Nile on a date ... and get totally extinguished. Fizzle!

HooDude Voodoo

Most likely to ... become a leading scareologist.

C.A. Cupid

Most likely to ... find Ms. Kindergrübber a boyfriend.

Sloman "Slo Mo" Mortavitch

Most likely to ... get there in the end!

....

Most likely to ... .

....

Heath's HALL OF FLAME

Heath Burns is one of Monster High's most hapless students ... so we couldn't resist inviting him to turn the tables on the teachers whose classes he routinely fails! Here are Heath's very own freaktacular faculty awards.

MR. HACKINGTON

MOST LIKELY TO ... ACCIDENTALLY DISSECT A STUDENT.

First prize

FOR HER FANGTASTIC DEVIL'S FOOD CAKE is awarded to MS. KINDERGRÜBBER.

1st

CERTIFICATE OF EXCELLENCE IN

GROWLING

ADVANCED LEVEL HORSE CARE AND MONSTROUS RIDING SKILLS

HEADMISTRESS BLOODGOOD

A

MR. ROTTER

SCARY APTITUDE TEST

RESULTS FOR
MR. WHERE

LEVEL 3 – VANISHING AND APPEARING AT WILL
LEVEL 6 – FIRST AID
...ILIZATION IN BANDAGES)

MR. D'EATH

SCARY-COOLEST MEMBER OF THE FACULTY, AS VOTED FOR BY THE STUDENT BODIES OF MONSTER HIGH

To each and every student body,

I am, as ever, immensely honored to be the headless head at the helm of this establishment. I never cease to walk through the howlways of Monster High and feel shivers of excitement run down my spine! After reading the record of your time here, I can see that you too are proud of your school, which is, as I often hear you say, "scary-cool." There truly is never a dull day being one of the undead on these premises!

Many thanks to the Fearbook team and congratulations to you all for your many clawsome achievements this year.

Headmistress
Bloodgood

BYE FROM THE HIGH!

C.A. Cupid

GFFs Forever Love
Frankie, Draculaura
and Clawdeen

All the beast for the future
~~Jackson Jekyll~~
xx

Abbey Bominable X

HOLT HYDE

SloMo

HOWDY FROM
HOWLEEN X

GROWL TO THE BEAT!
HOLT HYDE.

What a fangtastic
year we've had!
Rochelle x

HEATH
xxxxxx

Hope all your school days
are horrific, Toralei

Have a fearsome
year! Love
Venus McFlytrap

Here's howlin' at ya
Clawd Wolf

Nefera de Nile

(Keep this book 'cause my signature is going to be priceless one day!)

Robecca X

From Gil Webber

From one golden ghoul to another Cleo Xxxxx
P.S. Love and hisses from Hissette!

Purrsephone & Meowlody

Operetta
x

Peace and love from Lagoona Blue Xxx

Scream ya soon, Scarah X

DEUCE

Nnnnrrggggnnnggh
Ghoulia Yelps

Keep checking my blog for the latest ghostly goss. Spectra x

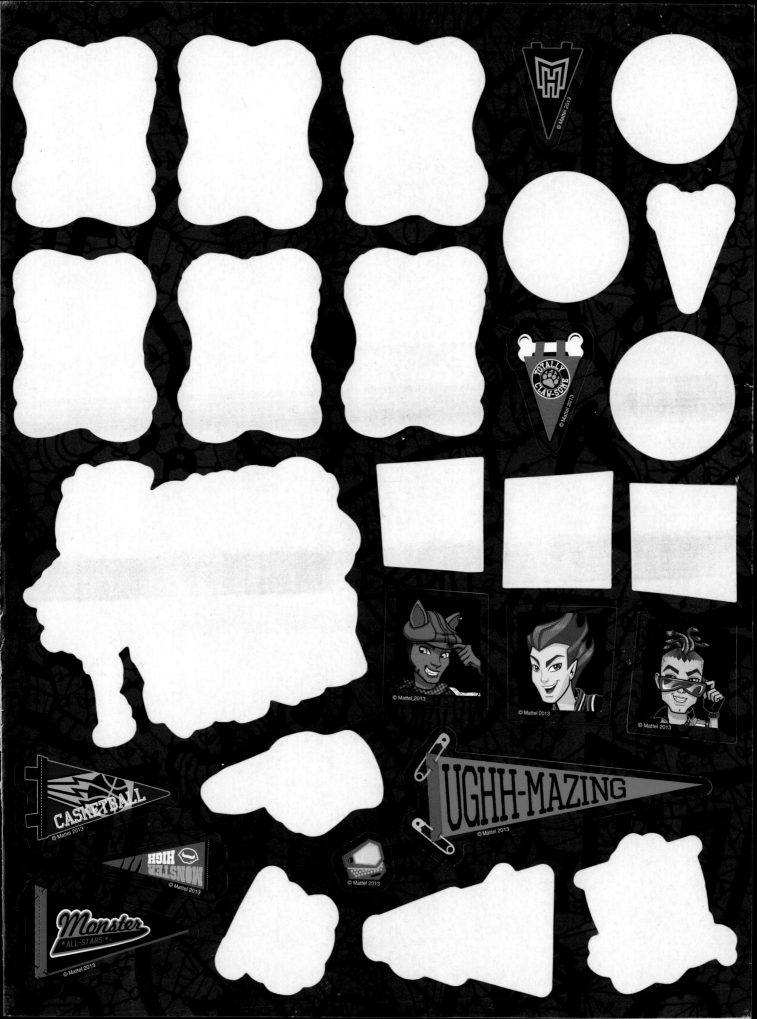